A Chair for My Mother

by *Vera B. Williams*

Greenwillow Books, New York

A Chair for My Mother
Copyright © 1982 by Vera B. Williams. All rights reserved.
Manufactured in China.
For information address HarperCollins
Children's Books, a division of
HarperCollins Publishers,
195 Broadway, New York, NY 10007.
www.harperchildrens.com
20 SCP 40 39 38 37 36 35

Library of Congress Cataloging-in-Publication Data

Williams, Vera B.
A chair for my mother.
"Greenwillow Books."
Summary: A child, her waitress mother,
and her grandmother save dimes to buy
a comfortable armchair after all their
furniture is lost in a fire.
[1. Family life—Fiction.
2. Saving and investment—Fiction.
3. Chairs—Fiction.]   I. Title.
PZ7.W6685Ch   [E]   81-7010
ISBN 0-688-00914-X   AACR2
ISBN 0-688-00915-8 (lib. bdg.)
ISBN 0-688-04074-8 (pbk.)

to the memory of my mother, Rebecca Poringer Baker

My mother works as a waitress in the Blue Tile Diner. After school sometimes I go to meet her there. Then her boss, Josephine, gives me a job too.

I wash the salts and peppers and fill the ketchups. One time I peeled all the onions for the onion soup. When I finish, Josephine says, "Good work, honey," and pays me. And every time, I put half of my money into the jar.

It takes a long time to fill a jar this big. Every day when my mother comes home from work, I take down the jar. My mama empties all her change from tips out of her purse for me to count. Then we push all of the coins into the jar.

Sometimes my mama is laughing when she comes home from work. Sometimes she's so tired she falls asleep while I count the money out into piles. Some days she has lots of tips. Some days she has only a little. Then she looks worried. But each evening every single shiny coin goes into the jar.

We sit in the kitchen to count the tips. Usually Grandma sits
with us too. While we count, she likes to hum. Often she has
money in her old leather wallet for us. Whenever she gets a
good bargain on tomatoes or bananas or something she buys,
she puts by the savings and they go into the jar.

When we can't get a single other coin into the jar, we are going to take out all the money and go and buy a chair.

Yes, a chair. A wonderful, beautiful, fat, soft armchair. We will get one covered in velvet with roses all over it. We are going to get the best chair in the whole world.

That is because our old chairs burned up. There was a big fire in our other house. All our chairs burned. So did our sofa and so did everything else. That wasn't such a long time ago.

My mother and I were coming home from buying new shoes. I had new sandals. She had new pumps. We were walking to our house from the bus. We were looking at everyone's tulips. She was saying she liked red tulips and I was saying I liked yellow ones. Then we came to our block.

Right outside our house stood two big fire engines. I could see lots of smoke. Tall orange flames came out of the roof. All the neighbors stood in a bunch across the street. Mama grabbed my hand and we ran. My uncle Sandy saw us and ran to us. Mama yelled, "Where's Mother?" I yelled, "Where's my grandma?" My aunt Ida waved and shouted, "She's here, she's here. She's O.K. Don't worry."

Grandma was all right. Our cat was safe too, though it took a while to find her. But everything else in our whole house was spoiled.

What was left of the house was turned to charcoal and ashes.

We went to stay with my mother's sister Aunt Ida and Uncle Sandy. Then we were able to move into the apartment downstairs. We painted the walls yellow. The floors were all shiny. But the rooms were very empty.

The first day we moved in, the neighbors brought pizza and cake and ice cream. And they brought a lot of other things too.

The family across the street brought a table and three kitchen chairs. The very old man next door gave us a bed from when his children were little.

My other grandpa brought us his beautiful rug. My mother's

other sister, Sally, had made us red and white curtains. Mama's
boss, Josephine, brought pots and pans, silverware and dishes.
My cousin brought me her own stuffed bear.

Everyone clapped when my grandma made a speech. "You
are all the kindest people," she said, "and we thank you very,
very much. It's lucky we're young and can start all over."

That was last year, but we still have no sofa and no big chairs. When Mama comes home, her feet hurt. "There's no good place for me to take a load off my feet," she says. When Grandma wants to sit back and hum and cut up potatoes, she has to get as comfortable as she can on a hard kitchen chair.

So that is how come Mama brought home the biggest jar she could find at the diner and all the coins started to go into the jar.

Now the jar is too heavy for me to lift down. Uncle Sandy gave me a quarter. He had to boost me up so I could put it in.

After supper Mama and Grandma and I stood in front of the jar. "Well, I never would have believed it, but I guess it's full," Mama said.

My mother brought home little paper wrappers for the nickels and the dimes and the quarters. I counted them all out and wrapped them all up.

On my mother's day off, we took all the coins to the bank. The bank exchanged them for ten-dollar bills. Then we took the bus downtown to shop for our chair.

We shopped through four furniture stores. We tried out big chairs and smaller ones, high chairs and low chairs, soft chairs and harder ones. Grandma said she felt like Goldilocks in "The Three Bears" trying out all the chairs.

Finally we found the chair we were all dreaming of. And the money in the jar was enough to pay for it. We called Aunt Ida and Uncle Sandy. They came right down in their pickup truck to drive the chair home for us. They knew we couldn't wait for it to be delivered.

I tried out our chair in the back of the truck. Mama wouldn't let me sit there while we drove. But they let me sit in it while they carried it up to the door.

We set the chair right beside the window with the red and white curtains. Grandma and Mama and I all sat in it while Aunt Ida took our picture.

Now Grandma sits in it and talks with people going by in the daytime. Mama sits down and watches the news on TV when she comes home from her job. After supper, I sit with her and she can reach right up and turn out the light if I fall asleep in her lap.